CLARE HARRIS

The Umbrella

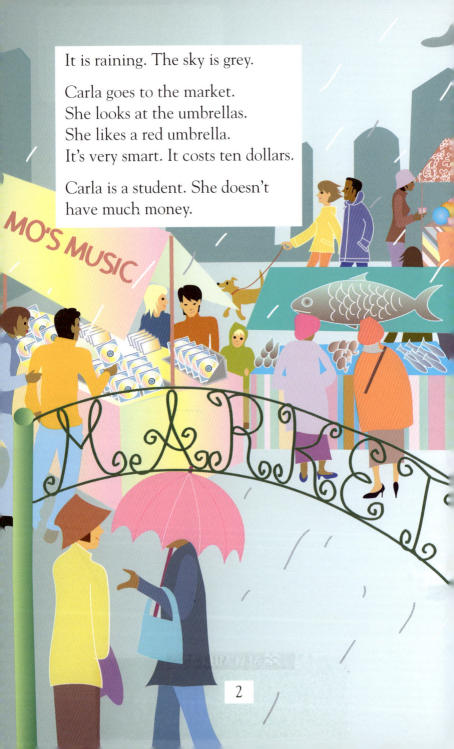

It is raining. The sky is grey.

Carla goes to the market.
She looks at the umbrellas.
She likes a red umbrella.
It's very smart. It costs ten dollars.

Carla is a student. She doesn't
have much money.

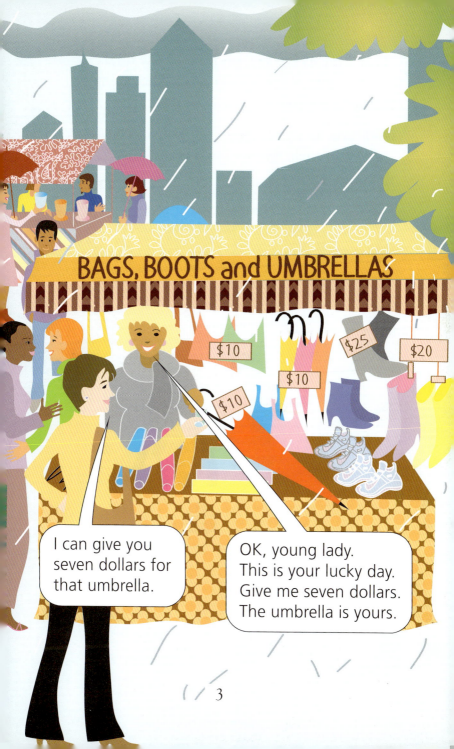

3

'This is my lucky day!' says Carla. She holds the red umbrella above her head. The rain falls on the umbrella.

Carla goes to a cake shop. She wants to buy some cakes. Her little brother loves cakes. She goes into the shop.

She leaves her red umbrella near the door.

CAROLINE'S CAKE SHOP

It is quiet inside the shop.

Carla chooses three small cakes.
She talks to the shop assistant.

A customer is leaving the shop.
She is a young woman. She is
holding a cake box.

Carla is going to leave the shop.
But where is her umbrella?

There is one umbrella near the door. It is
not a red umbrella. It is not Carla's umbrella.
This umbrella is old and black. It has
a pattern of yellow ducks. It is not smart.
Carla takes the umbrella.

This is not my lucky day!

CAROLIN

Carla walks to the town square.

A young man speaks to her.

Hello!

He smiles.
Carla does not know this young man.
She walks away quickly.

The young man is following Carla. She walks into a crowd of people. The young man follows the black and yellow umbrella.

Hello! Wait!

Carla turns. She looks
at the young man. She is
angry. 'Go away!' she says.

The young man is sad.

'Marisa, I'm sorry!' he says.
'I'm very late.'

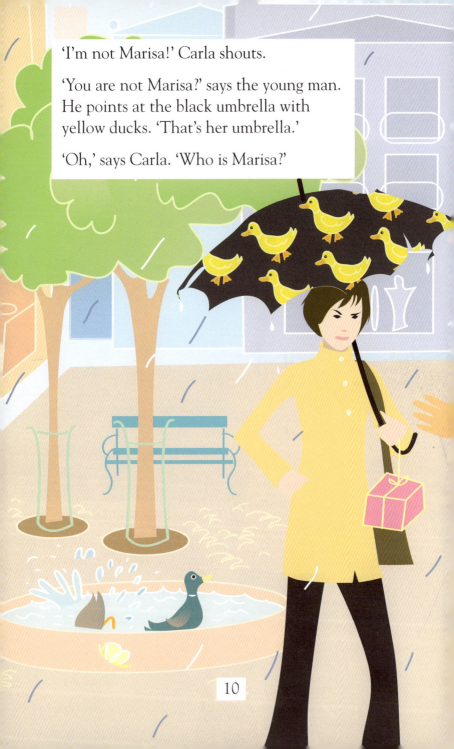

'I'm not Marisa!' Carla shouts.

'You are not Marisa?' says the young man. He points at the black umbrella with yellow ducks. 'That's her umbrella.'

'Oh,' says Carla. 'Who is Marisa?'

'I don't know Marisa,' says the young man. 'I'm going to meet her. We are going to have coffee. It is my cousin's idea. Marisa works with my cousin.'

'I am not Marisa!' says Carla again.

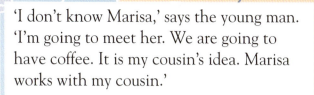

RESTAURANTE
LAS PARAGUAS

'My cousin has a photo of Marisa,' says the young man. 'She's tall. You're tall. Her hair is short and dark. Your hair is short and dark. In the photo, she has an umbrella. It's a black umbrella with yellow ducks. You have a black umbrella with yellow ducks!'

Carla looks up at the old umbrella. 'Marisa is a thief,' she thinks. 'She has my new red umbrella.' Carla is angry again.

'Please don't be angry,' says the young man. He looks at his watch. 'It's three o'clock. Marisa goes to work at 2.30. I can't meet her now. It's too late.'

12

He smiles at Carla. 'Let's have coffee together,' he says.

Carla thinks for a moment. 'OK,' she says. 'Let's go to my aunt's café.'

The young man smiles again. 'That will be great,' he says.

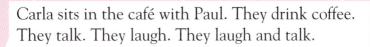

Carla sits in the café with Paul. They drink coffee.
They talk. They laugh. They laugh and talk.

Suddenly Carla jumps up.
'Oh, no!' she says. 'It's late. I must go home.
I must study. I'm going to have an exam tomorrow.'

14

It is almost dark. The town square is quiet.

Carla sees a tall young woman. The young woman has short dark hair. She has a smart umbrella. It is a red umbrella.

The young woman is Marisa!

Marisa sees the old black umbrella with yellow ducks. She is worried. Suddenly, her face is red.

'Don't worry,' says Carla. 'Keep my red umbrella. I like this umbrella. It's a lucky umbrella. This is my lucky day!'

The rain falls on the umbrellas. Carla smiles. Then she runs home.